AIDS AND HIV

Katie Dicker

New York

Published in 2011 by The Rosen Publishing Group, Inc.
29 East 21st Street, New York, NY 10010

First Edition

Senior Editor: Claire Shanahan
Designer: Phipps Design
Photo Researcher: Kath Kollberg
Proofreader and Indexer: Jo Kemp

Library of Congress Cataloging-in-Publication Data

Dicker, Katie.
AIDS and HIV / Katie Dicker.
    p. cm. -- (Global issues)
Includes bibliographical references and index.
ISBN 978-1-4488-1876-1 (library binding)
1. AIDS (Disease)--Juvenile literature. 2. HIV infections--
Juvenile literature. I. Title.
RC606.65.D53 2011
362.196'9792--dc22
                          2010023608

Photo Credits:
African Pictures: Shuter and Shooter p. 5 and cover, Eric Miller p. 6, p. 16, p. 17;
p. 12, Guy Stubbs p. 20. Corbis: Wendy Stone p. 7, David Turnley p. 21, Andrew
Brookes p. 27, Liu Haifeng/Xinhua Press p. 24, Polak Matthew p. 36, Reuters
p. 41, Gideon Mendel p. 33, Wyman IRA p. 34, Markus Moellenberg/zefa p. 43.
Getty Images: Hulton Archive p. 13, AFP p. 30. Reuters p. 4, p. 19, David Gray
p. 22, p. 40, p. 42. Rex Features: Francis Dean p. 9, Photoreporters Inc p. 14,
Sipa Press p. 29, p. 32, Nils Jorgensen p. 37, p. 38. Science Photo Library: J.C
Tessier, Publiphoto Diffusion p. 8, Eye of Science p. 10. Simon Roberts p. 18.
UNAIDS: G Pirozzi p. 25 and Cover, p. 28, Y Shimizu p. 44.

Manufactured in China
CPSIA Compliance Information: Batch #W11YA: For Further Information
Contact Rosen Publishing, New York, New York at 1-800-237-9932

Contents

Chapter 1
What Is AIDS?   **4**

Chapter 2
The History of AIDS   **8**

Chapter 3
AIDS Uncovered   **12**

Chapter 4
The Impact of AIDS   **18**

Chapter 5
The Battle with AIDS   **24**

Chapter 6
AIDS and the Media   **36**

Chapter 7
What Does the Future Hold?   **42**

Glossary   **46**

Further Information and Web Sites   **48**

Index   **48**

What Is AIDS?

On June 5, 1981, the world woke up to news reports of a new disease affecting gay men in the United States. Five homosexual men in Los Angeles had contracted a rare form of pneumonia. And before long, it became clear that gay men were not the only people affected.

A Mystery Disease

This was the beginning of our fight against AIDS, a disease caused by the Human Immunodeficiency Virus (HIV). Soon, a group of gay men in New York and San Francisco were found to have a new type of skin cancer, too. And when drug users

Today, HIV is found worldwide. We are all at risk—whatever age, gender, or skin color—and we must learn about ways to protect ourselves.

began to show similar symptoms, doctors realized the disease was spreading.

More than 25 years have passed and, despite huge advances in medical science, AIDS is now one of the most destructive diseases in history. Over 25 million people have died from AIDS since 1981, affecting nearly every country worldwide. This mystery disease affecting a few homosexual men in the U.S.A. has developed into the worst pandemic the world has ever faced.

What Is AIDS?

During the 1980s, tests revealed that HIV—a virus that weakens the immune system—was responsible for the mystery sickness. The disease was defined by the Centers for Disease Control and Prevention

(CDC) in Atlanta in 1982 and became known as AIDS (Acquired Immune Deficiency Syndrome). AIDS is a collection of rare illnesses that people with HIV can develop because their immune system is unable to fight against infection. But having HIV does not necessarily mean that you have AIDS.

AIDS is a fatal disease in many parts of the world. But new treatments and greater awareness are giving hope to people living with HIV.

are often dependent on someone's general health and their access to healthcare. However, new treatments mean that today most people living with HIV do not go on to develop AIDS.

What Are the Symptoms?

The symptoms of AIDS vary, but include fever, diarrhea, weight loss, swollen glands, or more serious infections and tumors. It can take years for HIV to damage the immune system so much that a person becomes unwell. But once someone has contracted AIDS, the average survival time is about a year. These estimates vary widely however, and

How Do You Get HIV?

HIV is spread by the exchange of infected body fluids—mainly through sexual activity or from the exchange of contaminated blood. Although HIV is most common in sub-Saharan Africa, nearly every country in the world is now affected. With increasing levels of HIV infection, everyone needs to take precautions to protect themselves.

 December 1983 In the U.S.A., the number of infections reaches 3,064, and deaths from the disease total 1,292 >>>

Is there a Cure?

There is currently no cure for AIDS, but treatments can slow the speed at which HIV damages the body, to prevent AIDS developing. If someone is diagnosed early, and responds well to treatment, they can lead a full and active life—with normal life expectancy.

Treatment Development

Research over the past 25 years has enabled scientists to understand more about the causes of HIV and the way the virus spreads. In the 1990s, the introduction of antiretroviral treatments brought hope to millions of people living with HIV. But it's a lifelong commitment: treatments have to be taken regularly; the drugs are very strong; and they can have unpleasant side effects. Recent developments, such as trials for an HIV vaccine and the introduction of microbicides, hope to revolutionize HIV treatment and prevention for future generations.

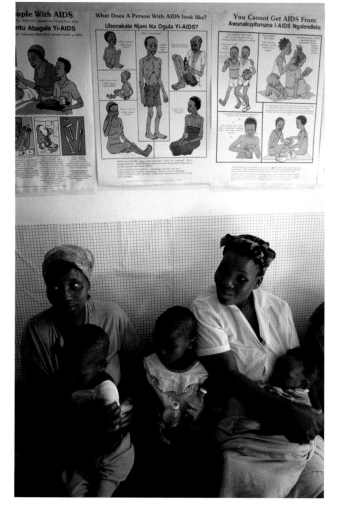

Women wait patiently for treatment at an AIDS clinic in Africa. Although antiretroviral treatments are now available, access is limited in many parts of the world.

Disease Destruction

Nevertheless, until effective treatments are available for all, the impact of AIDS is having a devastating effect. Families are losing loved ones, children are becoming orphans at a young age, and the financial impact of the disease is forcing many communities into poverty. These repercussions are affecting countries and continents, too. Health services are under strain, skilled workers are dying, and research into prevention and a possible cure is costing billions of dollars.

April 1984 Margaret Heckler, the U.S. Health and Human Services Secretary, announces the isolation of the virus that causes AIDS and claims a test could be available within six months and a vaccine within two years >>>

Why Is HIV Spreading?

HIV does not spread easily. Using a condom during sex and avoiding contact with infected blood are two simple preventative measures. The virus is also unable to survive outside the body for more than a few minutes. So why are more people becoming infected with HIV? The past 25 years have taught us that many political and social influences are affecting the crisis, too. Today, we travel around the world more than ever before, some people have more sexual partners, and despite the warnings, many people remain complacent about how easily they may get affected. In some countries, there is limited access to treatment. In others, problems of adherence are causing different strains of the virus to emerge. Stigma around HIV is also preventing people from getting tested, increasing the risk of the virus spreading.

QUOTE >

In the 1980s, fears about the cause of AIDS were very real. Princess Diana made headlines when she went to open the UK's first specialist AIDS hospital ward in 1987.

"She shook my hand without her gloves on. That proves you can't get AIDS from normal social contact."

A patient quoted in the Bureau of Hygiene & Tropical Diseases "AIDS Newsletter," April 10, 1987.

Although AIDS has been in the news for over 25 years, it has taken time for public health messages to get through. Straight Talk *is produced in Uganda to address issues of sex education for adolescents—one specialist publication that is proving effective.*

 March 1987 The U.S. Food and Drug Administration (FDA) approves azidothymidine (AZT) as the first antiretroviral drug for HIV >>>

January 1995 The CDC announces that AIDS has become the leading cause of death among Americans age 25–44 >>>

The History of AIDS

AIDS is not the first epidemic we have had to face. Major diseases of the past have also claimed millions of lives, devastating families, communities, and countries. But AIDS has brought a different challenge. While we struggle to contain the disease, we also know that—with the right precautions—future infections could be prevented.

Deadly Epidemics

Less than a hundred years ago, the Spanish flu (1918–1919) is thought to have taken over 50 million lives. In the

Some deadly diseases are difficult to control. Malaria is spread from the bite of infected female mosquitoes. The virus remains a killer because it constantly adapts to treatment.

fourteenth century, the Black Death killed around 25 million people. And more recently, in 2003, SARS and bird flu caused major scares around the world. Killer diseases are still at large and we are never free from risk. But with improving standards of healthcare, we are beginning to overcome the threat of most serious epidemics.

But the challenge of AIDS is different. It is not spread through casual contact and in theory should be easily overcome—unlike other diseases, HIV is not passed through the air, spread through dirty water, or transmitted by insects. But still, the threat is growing. What makes AIDS different from epidemics of the past is the range of political and social factors influencing its treatment and prevention.

May 1969 An African-American teenager, Robert, dies from a mystery illness, later confirmed as the first case of AIDS in the U.S.A. >>>

April 1976 Arvid Noe, a Norwegian sailor, and his wife and two-year-old child, die from a mystery illness that is later linked to AIDS >>>

In the modern world, it is not uncommon for people to travel to different countries—to take vacations, or to live and work. This brings a greater risk of catching diseases—and HIV is no exception.

The Early Years

Although AIDS was first reported in 1981, examples of HIV infection have now been identified as early as the 1960s. Scientists believe that HIV was transferred to humans in central Africa around 1930, when infected chimpanzees were slaughtered for meat. When a person with HIV then traveled to Haiti in the 1960s, the virus spread, and soon it reached the United States, too.

Although HIV was unheard of at the time, tests on tissue samples have now revealed that the virus was the cause of mystery deaths in the 1960s and 70s.

In 1969, for example, a teenager from St. Louis, Missouri, died from a rare form of cancer, and in 1976, a cancerous illness claimed the life of a Norwegian sailor. Doctors suspect he became infected with HIV in Cameroon, Africa, in the 1960s.

A Growing Concern

AIDS has now claimed over 25 million lives. What began as a localized problem in Africa, Haiti, and the U.S.A., has now spread to the far reaches of the globe. In 2008 alone, there were over 2 million deaths from AIDS and 2.5 million new HIV infections. What is even more worrying is that statistics do not tell the whole story. Scientists estimate, for example, that there are currently over 75,000 people living with HIV in the UK, a third of whom are undiagnosed.

1999 Researchers at the University of Alabama claim that a chimpanzee, once common in West Central Africa, is the source of HIV >>>

Case Study: Dr. James Curran, Task Force Coordinator for the CDC

On June 4, 1981, the Centers for Disease Control (CDC) published a paper in *Morbidity and Mortality Weekly Report* (MMWR) about cases of Pneumocystis carinii pneumonia (PCP) in five homosexual men in Los Angeles, California. This was the first published work to draw the world's attention to the as yet unknown disease called AIDS.

A colored electron microscope image of a selection of Human Immunodeficiency Viruses (HIV)—the cause of AIDS. HIV attacks white blood cells in the body's immune system.

Urgent Investigations

One month later, Dr. James Curran was appointed the coordinator of the CDC "Task Force on Kaposi's Sarcoma and Opportunistic Infections." For 15 years, he directed a team of researchers investigating the cause and nature of the disease and the most effective ways to protect people from infection.

Before long, newspapers began to report initial findings about the curious condition. Because so little was known about the disease, there were worries that it was contagious, or could be spread by people who had no apparent symptoms. Doctors were puzzled—Kaposi's Sarcoma (KS) was a cancer usually found in older people and, until that time, PCP was a rare lung infection.

Piecing the Jigsaw Together

The cause of the disease was unknown and there was no evidence to suggest it was contagious. And for the time being, the condition seemed to only affect homosexual men.

Speculation about the reasons why a homosexual lifestyle could cause such severe symptoms began to surface. Nearly all the men first affected were frequent users of recreational drugs called nitrite inhalants (or "poppers"). Some researchers thought this might be the key to the sporadic outbreaks.

But knowledge about the disease was changing fast—just five months later, in December 1981, PCP was found to affect a group of injecting drug users, and the condition was also reported in the UK. Researchers realized they had a long battle ahead.

July 1982 23 states in the U.S.A. report a total of 452 cases of AIDS to the CDC >>>

July 1982 There are reports of AIDS in Haitians, leading to speculation that the disease may have originated in Haiti >>>

WHAT THE WORLD THINKS...

These are four different publications commenting on the CDC's efforts in the 1980s. Compare and contrast the various viewpoints and see if you can find any more newspaper reports or other media discussing first documented cases of AIDS.

Michael S. Gottlieb, MMWR report, June 4, 1981

'The patients did not know each other and had no known common contacts...who had had similar diseases....Two of the 5 reported having frequent homosexual contacts with various partners. All 5 reported using inhalant drugs...'

Michael S. Gottlieb is the former assistant professor of medicine at the University of California, Los Angeles School of Medicine.

Pacific Stars and Stripes, June 8, 1981

"A parasite-caused pneumonia that killed two previously healthy men and infected three others may be linked to 'some aspect of a homosexual lifestyle,' [the CDC reports]. 'The fact that these patients were all homosexuals suggests an association between some aspect of a homosexual lifestyle or disease acquired through sexual contact.'"

Pacific Stars and Stripes is a newspaper published for the U.S. Armed Forces overseas. This extract comes from an edition published in Tokyo, Japan.

The Gettysburg Times, December 10, 1981

"The condition—so new it does not have a name—has been reported in 180 people in 15 states...and 73 of the victims have died. 'It is a very serious problem and does not seem to be on the wane,' said Dr. James Curran of the [CDC]. 'This is probably just the tip of the iceberg.'"

Dr. James Curran, CDC teleconference, May 5, 2006

"It is sometimes difficult to reflect 25 years, going back to five cases of pneumocystis in gay men in June of 1981, to understand how something that began so slowly and so quietly, can now be the number four cause of death in the entire world, something that we thought was a small problem back then...I think we still have to consider that we may be underestimating the burden and impact of this insidious [subtley yet harmfully spreading] global epidemic..."

December 1982 The CDC reports the first cases of HIV passing from mother to child >>>

AIDS Uncovered

We now know more about the origins of HIV and we've come to understand how the virus spreads. But scientists and social researchers are still baffled by increasing levels of infection. HIV prevention may look easy on paper, but in practice, too many lives are still at risk.

Two strains of HIV have been identified, known as HIV-1 (from the Central Common Chimpanzee) and HIV-2 (from the Sooty Mangabey monkey).

The Origins of HIV

Scientists now believe that HIV originated from human contact with chimpanzees and monkeys in Africa. Tests have revealed cases of a similar virus called Simian Immunodeficiency Virus (SIV) affecting these primates. SIV mutated to a human form, causing the symptoms of AIDS to develop in humans. But scientists have yet to discover why SIV-infected animals have not developed symptoms of this kind.

Local Problems

Although HIV is a worldwide problem, the way the virus spreads in each country often varies. In Ukraine, for example, drug users were the first to be affected. The initial outbreak in the U.S.A. and the UK was largely limited to homosexual and bisexual relations, while in sub-Saharan Africa, heterosexual relations have been vulnerable to infection from the beginning. Today, with the spread of the virus reaching pandemic proportions, the disease is no longer confined to any particular group of society.

Unprotected Sex

Despite variations between countries, the main cause of HIV transmission worldwide is unprotected sex. The use of a condom—although not 100 percent effective—is a universal method of prevention. In the West, condoms are widely available and in most cases, unprotected sex is a choice. But, in other countries, access to condoms is limited. The use of contraception has clashed with religious beliefs and culture, too. Many African communities, for instance, oppose the use of condoms.

The Catholic Church has also long opposed the use of contraception. But in recent years, talks between the World Health Organization (WHO) and the Vatican are bringing hope that barrier contraception will be supported in the fight against HIV.

Blood Protection

In the 1980s, blood transfusions transmitted HIV in some cases. Today, in most countries, donated blood is tested and heat-treated to protect patients from the virus and medical staff wear latex gloves as a routine measure. Sterilized needles are now also offered to drug users, and recommended for practices such as tattoos and body piercing, to prevent the virus spreading via contaminated needles.

HIV can also be passed from a mother to child, during the last stages of pregnancy, at childbirth, or while breastfeeding. Mothers with HIV can now reduce this risk, however, by using antiretroviral drugs during pregnancy, by having a Caesarean birth, and by bottle-feeding their child.

Most of the 2 million children living with HIV in sub-Saharan Africa became infected from their mother during pregnancy or through breastfeeding.

 1994 A large European study shows that Caesarean births halve the rate of HIV transmission between mother and child >>>

Case Study: The Ray Brothers, HIV-Positive from Contaminated Blood

In 1986, a family from Arcadia, Florida, was at the center of a national controversy in the U.S.A. when the DeSoto County School Board banned their sons from attending classes because they had HIV.

Fear in the Community

Ricky, Robert, and Randy Ray contracted HIV through blood products used to treat their hemophilia. They were diagnosed in 1986 at 7, 8, and 9 years of age. When the family were ostracized by the local community, they moved to Alabama. But when school records were transferred, the boys were banned from their classes in Alabama, too.

The family moved back to Arcadia to fight their cause. They sued the DeSoto County School Board and in August 1987, won the right for the boys to attend school. But the discrimination continued. A local group called Citizens Against AIDS in Schools urged parents to keep their children at home. Bomb threats forced the temporary closure of the boys' school, Memorial Elementary, and a week after the court decision, the Ray's home was burned down. Police suspected arson, but the case was never proved.

Raising Awareness

In 1988, the family moved to Sarasota and began to campaign for greater awareness and understanding of HIV and AIDS. They spoke to groups across the United States and appeared on national radio and television shows.

In 1992, Ricky died—he was 15. But the family's continued activism saw the Ricky Ray Relief Fund Act passed in 1998. This law allows the U.S. government to compensate hemophiliacs who contracted HIV between 1982 and 1987. Robert died in 2000, age 22. Randy has been successfully controlling his symptoms using modern treatments.

Ricky and Robert Ray lost their lives because of contaminated blood used to treat their hemophilia. But their legacy lives on.

October 1985 All blood transfusion centers in the UK begin routine testing of blood donations for HIV >>>

August 28, 1987 The Ray's family home is set on fire. No one is prosecuted >>>

WHAT THE WORLD THINKS...

These are three different publications commenting on the Ray brothers. Compare and contrast the various viewpoints and see if you can find any more newspaper reports or other media discussing the Ray family and their impact on AIDS education.

Facts on File News Services web site, September 4, 1987

"The fire capped a week of bomb and death threats against the Ray family, and a boycott of local schools. The boycott had been prompted by the Aug. 24 return to school of the three boys after a year's absence.

"Louise Ray said that her family would leave DeSoto County. 'I never thought it would go this far,' she said.

"The family's plight…attracted national attention, and offers of aid were pouring in from across the country. A family spokesman… indicated that the Rays wanted any donations from DeSoto County to go toward efforts to educate the community about AIDS."

Miami Herald, December 14, 1992

"AIDS-infected Florida teenager Ricky Ray…died peacefully Sunday at his Orlando home. He was 15.

"His family will continue his efforts to educate others about AIDS and fight for a cure, Louise Ray said. Her son had 'wanted people to understand AIDS is not just this word that happens to somebody else—it can happen to everybody.'

"'Things changed so much for us around the country after the Ray family. People saw that education is really an imperative in dealing with AIDS,' said Alan Brownstein, executive director of the National Hemophilia Foundation in New York."

St. Petersburg Times, September 2, 2001

"Louise Ray had an epiphany the other day. She was visiting with a cousin here…and they were chatting about someone in town who is HIV-positive. They didn't speak in hushed tones or worried voices.

"And I thought, 'Boy, have things changed,'" she says. 'You couldn't have had that conversation 10, 15 years ago. Now, as a general rule, having HIV has become more acceptable. You're not considered a leper to be cast away anymore.'"

1989 The UK government announces it will pay £42 million ($63 million) compensation to hemophiliacs who have been infected with HIV from contaminated blood products >>>

1993 Tennis star Arthur Ashe dies from AIDS. It is thought he contracted HIV from a blood transfusion in 1983 >>>

HIV Antibody Testing

When a person is tested for HIV, a small blood sample is usually taken from a vein in the arm. The test measures the amount of CD4+ T cells in the blood—antibodies caused by the body's response to HIV. When a person becomes infected, it can take up to three months for the antibodies to develop. If a person has contracted the virus, we say they are HIV-positive (but this actually means they are HIV antibody-positive).

HIV tests measuring antibodies in a patient's urine or oral fluid are now available. They are often used in home-testing kits because they don't require the use of needles.

Treatment

Today, treatments for HIV can control the virus and delay the onset of AIDS in most cases. Highly active antiretroviral therapy (or HAART) was introduced in 1996. This usually involves a combination of three or more treatments—the drugs cannot kill HIV completely, but they help to stop the virus spreading in the body.

Antiretroviral drugs have to be taken regularly, as prescribed, to be effective. If a dose is missed, there is less medication in the body and a risk that the virus will reproduce. Different strains of the virus that are resistant to treatment may also develop, meaning another combination of treatments has to be tried. New treatments are being developed all the time, but the nature of the virus is also changing.

PEP Treatments

If someone thinks they have been exposed to HIV, Post Exposure Prophylaxis (PEP) can reduce the likelihood of the virus attacking the body. This treatment was first introduced in 1996, for healthcare workers coming into contact with HIV-infected blood. The use of PEP is controversial, but the treatment may become more widely available in the future. The drugs have to be taken within 72 hours of suspected infection and continued for four weeks. There are also side effects, such as headaches, fatigue, diarrhea, and vomiting, and a risk of liver or kidney damage in the long run.

June 1998 A Post Exposure Prophylaxis (PEP) program begins in San Francisco, California, to treat people who have recently been infected with HIV >>>

July 1998 The first case of HIV resistance to antiretroviral drugs is reported in San Francisco >>>

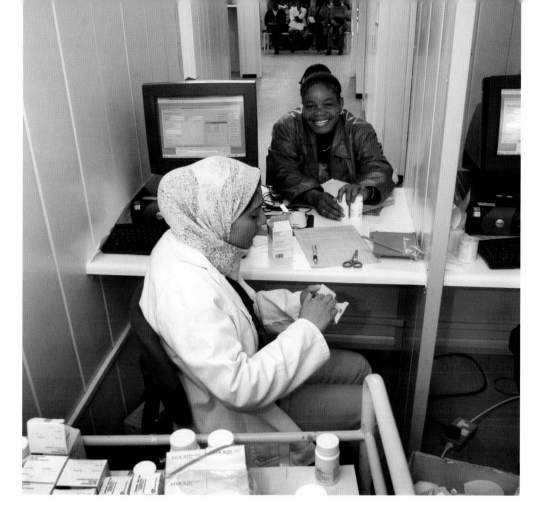

Antiretroviral treatments are now improving the lives of many people living with HIV.

A Vaccine for HIV?

Vaccinations encourage the immune system to create resistance to a virus. A safe and effective vaccine would hold the key to stemming the spread of HIV, with the potential to save millions of lives. It would potentially cost less than current treatments and would also overcome problems of adherence. But a vaccine is proving difficult to find. One difficulty is that HIV attacks the immune system—the very thing that

a vaccine is trying to activate. The nature of the virus is also constantly changing, making it difficult to find treatments that remain effective.

 1999 The UK government announces pregnant women will be offered an HIV test to reduce the number of babies infected with HIV >>>

The Impact of AIDS

When someone is diagnosed with HIV, they are not the only ones whose life changes. The virus is, of course, most serious to the health of the individual concerned, but the repercussions on friends and family—and even countries—can also be huge.

Human Costs

Imagine being told that you have a serious virus, and that, unless you take medication for the rest of your life, you are at risk of developing a deadly disease. Imagine trying to share this news with your friends and relatives, with a prospective employer, or with a partner at the start of a new relationship. It can't be easy. But this is the reality for over 33 million people currently living with HIV.

A diagnosis of HIV can cause some people to feel isolated. Others face discrimination or are at risk of losing their income. At its worst, HIV can lead to a loss of life. Every death to AIDS is one too many, and the effects are also devastating for those left behind. In Less Economically Developed Countries (LEDCs) in particular, the death of a parent brings financial insecurity, and the increasing number of children orphaned by AIDS—currently 12 million in Africa, for example—is a major concern.

An HIV-patient—Shimmer Gunda (age 26)—lies in a church hospital in Zimbabwe. The effects of HIV are fatal for many people living in Less Economically Developed Countries.

Economic Impact

Billions of dollars have been invested in the race to prevent HIV from spreading. It's an undeniably worthwhile cause, but it comes at a hefty price. In 2004, economists predicted an investment of $27 billion could prevent around 30 million new HIV infections —but what of the 33 million people already infected? Many countries, such as the U.S.A. and UK, have committed to providing access to HIV prevention, treatment, care, and support.

2001 India is reported to have the largest number of AIDS orphans in the world—1.2 million >>>

2002 The number of children orphaned by AIDS reaches 13.4 million >>>

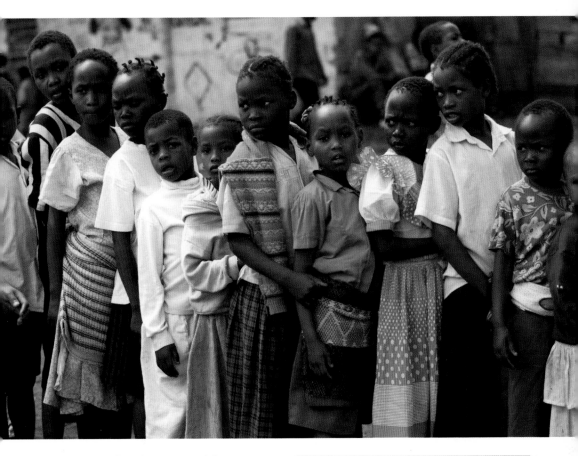

In sub-Saharan Africa, it is estimated that 9 percent of children have lost at least one of their parents to AIDS.

But if HIV infections continue to increase at the current rate, this will not be affordable.

In countries that have a fragile economic base, deaths from AIDS can slow economic growth still further. The pandemic puts pressure on healthcare resources and workers may need time off to care for their loved ones. Skilled workers may be lost to the disease—and if tax revenues are cut, other services such as education and healthcare come under additional strain.

QUOTE >

"AIDS destroys families, decimates communities, and, particularly in the poorest areas of the world, threatens to destabilize the social, cultural, and economic fabric of entire nations."

Rabbi David Saperstein, Director of the Religious Action Center of Reform Judaism.

 2002 Botswana becomes the first African country to provide free antiretroviral treatment. The program is expected to cost $24.5 million in the first year >>>

Stigma

HIV is not a visible condition and many people living with the virus find it difficult to talk about the disease. When someone is first diagnosed, there are real fears about job security, the reaction of partners and friends, and quality of life in the future.

Stigma creates the ideal conditions for HIV to spread. If someone with HIV avoids being tested or seeking advice about their sexual health, they risk passing the disease on to someone else. Stigma is fueled by fear and ignorance and education is therefore vital to prevent misunderstandings and discrimination against those affected.

In some countries in Africa, children with HIV are denied access to schooling or healthcare. Children who have lost their parents to AIDS may also be wrongly-assumed to have HIV themselves.

Types of Discrimination

In some countries, medical staff have refused treatment to people with HIV. Elsewhere, insurance policies have required a compulsory HIV test, and gay men have been refused health and life insurance regardless of their HIV status. Landlords have evicted HIV-positive tenants from their homes, and teachers and pupils have been dismissed from school because of an irrational fear they might transmit HIV to others.

1985 Ryan White, a 13-year-old American hemophiliac with HIV, is banned from school >>>

May 1988 The U.S. government distributes 107 million copies of a booklet called "Understanding AIDS" as part of a new education campaign >>>

Antidiscrimination laws, such as the Disability Discrimination Act 2005 in the UK, are helping cases of this kind, but sometimes they are not interpreted correctly. The stigma of HIV also reaches beyond those living with the condition— family, friends, and carers can be a target, too.

Reinforced Prejudice

The stigma surrounding HIV is often linked to other types of discrimination, such as racism or homophobia. In some countries, the gay or black community is an easy target for misinformed views. Inaccurate and biased media reports of HIV have enhanced this situation. Stigma is also apparent in what is not said—in the stories that don't get reported, because there are other, more grabbing headlines to feature.

Women's Rights

In 2006, almost 60 percent of adults living with HIV in sub-Saharan Africa were women. Studies have revealed that attitudes toward women is one factor causing HIV to spread. Some women are at risk of sexual assault or physical abuse if they disclose their HIV status. They may also have limited access to education, making them more vulnerable to infection. Condom use is not widespread in many African nations, and women are often unable to insist on barrier protection. Female condoms give greater control, but availability is limited and their cost can be prohibitive, particularly to those living in LEDCs.

While the world unites in the fight against AIDS, the disease is also associated with stigma and discrimination. Those living with HIV can feel marginalized by society.

QUOTE >

"What do I care for a disease that may kill me in 5–10 years when I know I won't have anything to eat tomorrow if I insist on condom use with my client?"

Sangita, 14, commercial sex worker, India, as quoted in UNDP's Regional Human Development Report, 2003.

May 1996 The U.S. Food and Drug Administration (FDA) approves the first "home sampling" tests for HIV >>>

Case Study: Margaret Marabe, an AIDS Campaigner in Papua New Guinea

In August 2007, Margaret Marabe spoke to reporters in Papua New Guinea, claiming she had seen AIDS patients being buried alive. Margaret was a campaigner working for Igat Hope [I've Got Hope], a volunteer organization. She had spent five months raising awareness of HIV and AIDS in the remote southern highlands of Papua New Guinea, a country in the eastern half of the Pacific island of New Guinea.

Women and children living with HIV secure refuge at a safe house in Papua New Guinea because their lives are in danger.

Lack of Awareness

Margaret claimed that poorly-educated families turned to such desperate measures because they could no longer look after their relatives and were terrified of being infected. She stressed the importance of extending AIDS awareness programs to rural areas, where ignorance of the disease was widespread.

Speculation about the basis of these stories mounted. Some attributed the tale to a lack of understanding in rural communities, where "victims" were marginalized and had no hope of accessing treatment. Others thought the reports revealed cultural practices in a region where euthanasia was unacceptable. There was also talk of a culture that regarded people with AIDS as the victims of witchcraft.

A Growing Crisis

Margaret's claims supported the United Nations' (UN's) reports warning that Papua New Guinea was facing an AIDS catastrophe. Officials claimed the mix of cultures and languages in the country was making it difficult to convey important public health messages.

In September 2007, an official investigation declared that Marabe's claims were unfounded. But the fact remains that the stigma of HIV is still very real after more than 25 years. And Papua New Guinea is not the only country affected. Growing suicide rates among those affected by HIV in India, for example, show just how important it is to address dangerous misconceptions that are costing lives.

WHAT THE WORLD THINKS...

These are four different publications commenting on Margaret Marabe's claims that AIDS patients were buried alive in Papua New Guinea. Compare and contrast the various viewpoints and see if you can find any more newspaper reports or other media discussing the investigation.

Daily Telegraph, UK, August 31, 2007

"[Burying relatives alive] is seen as the safest option. [They believe] if they killed the victims with a machete it would expose them to infection.

"Villagers' faith in Western medicine has been eroded in 32 years since independence from Australia by a decline in the public health system. Tribes often lay the blame for AIDS on 'witches,' who are tortured and killed."

International Herald Tribune, August 28, 2007

"Police and health workers in Papua New Guinea were investigating unverified claims...that people with AIDS were buried alive by their relatives. 'I saw three people with my own eyes,' [said Marabe]. 'When they got very sick and people could not look after them, they buried them.'

"...[P]olice and health workers were being sent to the Southern Highlands to investigate the claims...the stigma against people with HIV [is] very strong in the countryside, where education about the disease is scarce."

Kaiser Daily HIV/AIDS Report, Henry J. Kaiser Family Foundation, September 13, 2007

"The AIDS Committee of Papua New Guinea's Southern Highlands province has found no evidence that people living with HIV/AIDS in the area were buried alive...

"The media report sent wrong signals to everyone, including the international community here and abroad, who are funding HIV/AIDS programs in the country."

The Independent, UK, August 28, 2007

"...[Marabe] said, 'Why are they doing that?' And they said, 'If we let them live, stay in the same house, eat together, and use or share utensils, we will contract the disease and we too might die.'"

June 2006 In India, a 15-year-old boy sets himself on fire and commits suicide because of the stigma he faces having parents with HIV >>>

December 2006 The WHO predicts that one in five men, women, and children in Papua New Guinea will be infected within a decade >>>

23

The Battle with AIDS

The fight against AIDS is a global concern, but every country has its own way of dealing with the problem. International organizations try to coordinate the effort, but concerted action isn't always easy. Governments have different policies and priorities, situations change, and financial restraints invariably overshadow the good work that is being done.

A Worldwide Initiative

Statistics show that Africa bears the brunt of the AIDS epidemic. It knows more than any other continent about the real impact of HIV and AIDS. Around 65 percent of all HIV cases are in sub-Saharan Africa, and almost 90 percent of children with HIV are living there. But poverty forces these countries to turn to the West for support. Although aid and investment are urgently needed, problems arise because supporting countries often have little contact with those most affected.

Access to Information

In the Western world, public health campaigns have helped to make a difference. In the early days of the epidemic, blanket media coverage permeated all strands of society and AIDS became a recognized disease very quickly. Sex education programs began to advise communities, sexual health clinics encouraged HIV testing and offered support, and blood products were screened. But in LEDCs, this transfer of information was not so easily achieved. The limitations of poverty, education, and cultural practice simply prevented many public health messages getting through.

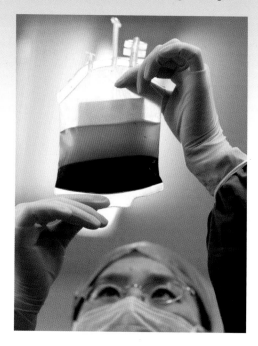

Since 1985, blood products in the Western world have been screened for HIV antibodies and heat-treated to protect patients from infection. This practice is gradually spreading around the world—but in some cases, not soon enough.

Getting the Message Across

Studies show that in many parts of Africa, community-based sex education is the most effective. Although messages need to be conveyed, people also like to take part in the decisions that affect their lives.

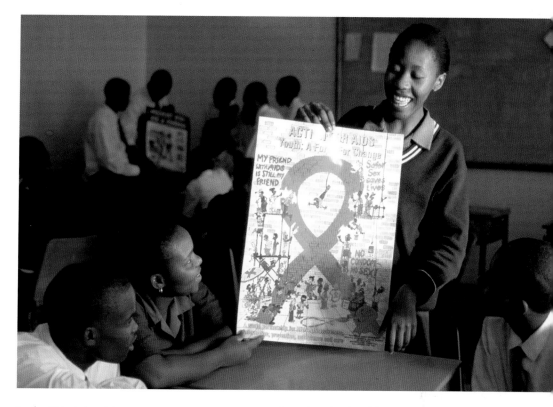

Sex education in African communities is helping to get important messages to a new generation. But resources are limited, and access to support for those living with HIV is proving inadequate.

In the West, healthcare messages are more readily accepted. But there is now a concern that sex education in schools and mass public awareness campaigns about HIV have declined in recent years. An element of complacency has set in, despite the fact that HIV is as widespread as ever. This rings true particularly in the U.S.A. and UK, where, despite additional resources, both homosexual and heterosexual HIV infections are rising. Studies have shown that many young people do not fear catching the deadly disease. This may be because drugs have made the disease less life threatening, or because they have not been faced with alarming publicity campaigns, such as those of the 1980s.

Effective Treatment

Most people with HIV in the Western world have access to treatment, but even then, side effects can cause problems of adherence. In LEDCs, only 8 percent of people living with HIV are currently able to access—and afford—life-saving drugs. In these countries, clean needles are in short supply and inadequate training is causing standards of sterilization to slip. A lack of proper nutrition is also causing those who have yet to receive medication to develop AIDS very quickly.

1987 An advertising campaign in the UK, "AIDS: Don't Die of Ignorance," sees leaflets delivered to every household and television ads warning people about the dangers of HIV >>>

March 1993 South Africa reports that HIV infections are expected to double that year >>>

Routine Testing

HIV antibody testing is vital if we are to overcome the AIDS crisis. Studies have shown that less than 1 percent of the sexually-active urban population in Africa has been tested, for example. And the figure is even lower in rural areas. Free voluntary testing and counseling services are now being offered to help those who cannot pay for health services.

In India, too, mobile HIV counseling and testing units are traveling to remote villages to offer support. In the West, home sampling tests are encouraging more people to take control of their sexual health. But there have been concerns about the accuracy of these tests, and the lack of counseling for those infected.

QUOTE >

Treatments are the key to reducing the impact of HIV, but prevention also relies on people taking control of their sexual health.

"We shouldn't pretend that we can give injections and work our way out of this. We have to change behavior, attitudes, and it has to be done in an organized, disciplined, systematic way."

Former U.S. President **Bill Clinton**, Keynote Address to the National Summit on Africa, February 17, 2000.

Microbicides

Microbicides are a method of prevention aimed particularly at women. These gels and creams act like an "invisible condom" preventing the transmission of HIV during sex. The treatments are designed to enhance the body's natural defenses to stop the virus from spreading to cells. Microbicides have the potential to save the lives of millions of women who are unable to insist on condom use—these women could use a microbicide without their partner knowing, for instance. Microbicides may take up to a decade to develop—they need to be safe, effective, affordable, and easy to administer—but these new treatments could revolutionize the prevention of HIV infections.

Alternative Treatments

Massage, stress management, and herbal remedies are just some of the treatments that were explored before antiretroviral drugs became available. More recently, vitamin and mineral supplements have been found to stem the virus in some people—a low-cost intervention that could offer hope in the early stages of infection. Other alternative ideas, however, are more alarming. A study of 260 African truck drivers, for example, showed that over a third believed that sleeping with a virgin was one cure for the disease.

In 2006, a scientific study found that male circumcision almost halved the risk of HIV infection among heterosexual men in Africa. This practice may now

1987 The Soviet Union (USSR) reports its first case of HIV, and tests for the virus are conducted across the country >>>

1992 Scientists explore the first microbicides that could safely prevent the transmission of HIV during sex >>>

26

Although HIV treatments are helping to stem the virus, they are expensive, access may be limited, and side effects are causing problems of adherence. Investment in new technologies, such as vaccines and microbicides, are now offering alternative strategies for the future.

be recommended in many of the countries worst affected by HIV, although cultural beliefs make it an unpopular option for many. There are also concerns that alternative theories of this kind encourage risk-taking behavior.

Natural Immunity?

In 2006, scientists in Boston, Massachusetts, began researching findings that some people had a natural resistance to HIV infection. There have been increasing numbers of people living with HIV whose immune system has somehow suppressed the virus so they remain healthy and symptom-free, without treatment. An understanding of how this process works could lead to entirely new drugs in the future.

November 1999 An early research study claims that male circumcision can help reduce rates of HIV infection in Africa and Asia >>>

Competing Priorities

AIDS is life threatening, but in a world where governments have to constantly address conflicting priorities with limited budgets, it's rarely at the top of the agenda. And in LEDCs, poverty forces other issues, such as education and employment—or basic needs such as drinking water and nutrition—to take priority. Governments also know that AIDS policies are not a natural vote winner, when so many short-term priorities are vying for attention.

Obstructive Policies

But when political leaders deny there is an AIDS problem, government inaction goes one step too far. In South Africa, for example, President Mbeki famously claimed that, although HIV could contribute to AIDS, other factors such as

There are now over 3,000 AIDS organizations working worldwide. These groups provide vital education and support to people living with HIV—helping to fill the gap of inadequate government intervention.

poverty and poor nutrition were to blame. South Africans did not have access to antiretroviral treatments until 2003 and the country now has one of the highest rates of HIV in the world. In 2006, more than 11 percent of South Africa's population had HIV—with estimates that by 2015, over 5.4 million South Africans could die from AIDS.

Denying the Risks

For many years, China regarded AIDS as a disease caused by contact with the West. They called it the "loving capitalism disease" and the government underplayed

 1991 In South Africa, the number of HIV infections among heterosexuals overtakes the number transmitted through homosexual relationships >>>

1997 Brazil is the first LEDC to begin providing free antiretroviral treatment >>>

the severity of the situation. In 1996, 4,500 cases of HIV infection were reported, but in reality, China was thought to have up to 100,000 infections.

In 2001, China finally admitted that the AIDS crisis needed addressing. The outbreak of SARS, in 2003, also revealed the dangers of not responding to an emerging epidemic. Public health initiatives have now been set up across the country, but the detention of AIDS activists is confusing the sentiment of the government's efforts.

In 2009, China reported that AIDS had become the country's leading cause of death among infectious diseases for the first time ever. During 2007, around 39,000 people died from AIDS. These statistics must be put into context though since China's population already exceeds 1.3 billion.

Lessons Learned

In other countries, government support has seen major success. In 2004, for example, a study revealed that the number of HIV infections in Uganda had fallen from 1.5 million to 0.5 million in a decade, largely thanks to the government's encouragement of health awareness and open communication. Government-sponsored medical research also highlighted the problem, reinforcing messages from the international community. As a result, there was a marked drop in the progression of the epidemic.

AIDS prevention posters such as this one displayed in a Beijing hospital are now widespread in China's cities. But for many years, the government failed to address the problems of HIV.

November 1999 China broadcasts its first television commercial for condoms in an effort to stop the spread of sexually transmitted diseases and HIV. The commercial is banned shortly afterward >>>

Case Study: Thabo Mbeki, the South African President

South Africa is one of the countries most severely affected by AIDS. In 2006, an estimated 5.5 million South Africans were living with HIV, and there were almost 1,000 deaths from AIDS every day.

Slow to Respond
While the rest of the world tried to address the challenges of HIV and AIDS through the 1980s and 90s, South Africa failed to provide a serious response to the crisis. The government began to supply antiretroviral treatments in 2003 after intense political pressure—but even then, only a third of patients were receiving treatment by 2007. And almost a third of pregnant women had HIV, giving birth to a new generation of infected children.

The Difficulties of a Nation
HIV infection in South Africa grew most rapidly at a time when the government was preoccupied with the abolition of apartheid. But when attention finally turned to the AIDS epidemic, intervention measures proved ineffective. The stigma of HIV, often associated as a disease of the poor, meant that many South Africans avoided testing. Women in particular feared physical abuse and a loss of economic security if their partner left them due to their HIV status. And public health

messages were failing to get through to a country that had literacy levels of just 14 percent, 11 official languages, and many isolated rural areas.

Thabo Mbeki's attitude toward the fight against AIDS have caused outrage in the international community.

Controversial Policies
When President Thabo Mbeki spoke at the International AIDS Conference in Durban in 2000, he famously inferred that poverty was the root cause of the epidemic, having worked with scientists who rejected the link between HIV and AIDS. Political pressure grew and in 2006, the government agreed to improve access to treatment. Thankfully, the epidemic is beginning to stabilize—but the effects of inaction have already denied hope to a generation.

October 1987 U.S. scientist Dr. Peter Duesberg publishes a report questioning the link between HIV and AIDS >>>

1999 South African President Thabo Mbeki claims the HIV-drug AZT is toxic and could be a danger to health >>>

WHAT THE WORLD THINKS...

These are three different publications commenting on the plight of AIDS in South Africa and the repercussions of his views. Compare and contrast the various viewpoints and see if you can find any more newspaper reports or other media discussing AIDS in South Africa.

The Daily Herald, Pennsylvania, November 18, 1991

"Scientists cite numerous reasons for the AIDS plague [in South Africa] including sexual promiscuity, poor medical services, the subservient role of women, war, and famine.

"Some blacks in South Africa even see the virus as a plot by whites to preserve apartheid by persuading blacks to use condoms, thus reducing the pregnancy rate in the black population."

European Stars and Stripes, Germany, July 26, 1999

"...[L]ife-extending AIDS drugs are out of the reach of the average South African. In a nation that is grappling with economic inequalities inherited from the apartheid regime, per capita GDP is [US]$4,400 a year. Meanwhile, name-brand AIDS drugs produced in Western nations such as the United States cost as much as $12,000 a year."

Waterloo Cedar Falls Courier, Iowa, July 14, 2000

"David Ho, one of the world's leading AIDS researchers, stood in front of thousands of experts at the International AIDS conference and made a statement that few would have thought necessary a few months ago: 'HIV is the cause of AIDS'....

Fears [that] President Thabo Mbeki's recent flirtation with fringe AIDS theories has...pushed many AIDS researchers and activists to take a stand on what has long been considered a closed issue.

"'Failure to properly address the modern plague caused by HIV disease is an act of irresponsibility that will be judged harshly by history,' [said Hoosen Coovadia, the chair or the International AIDS Conference in Durban]. 'President Mbeki, I beg you not to allow your legacy to be defined by inaction on this human catastrophe.'"

> **July 2000** In opposition to Mbeki's views, over 5,000 scientists around the world sign the "Durban Declaration" to support the view that HIV is the cause of AIDS >>>

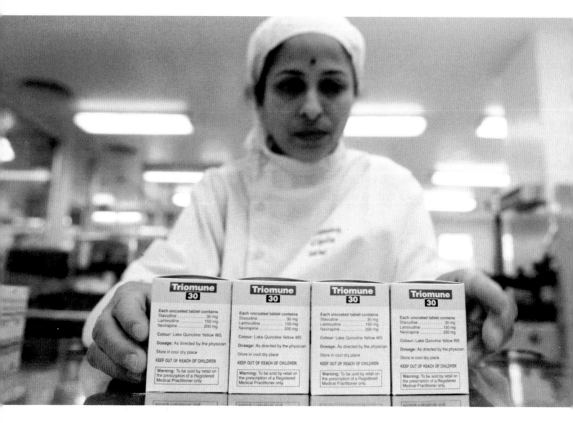

Pharmaceutical Profiteering

Pharmaceutical companies have long been accused of cashing in on the fight against AIDS. In 1989, for example, revelations that the drug AZT could slow the progression of HIV saw the value of Burroughs Wellcome, the company behind the drug, rise by 32 percent. But the cost of AZT remained prohibitive to many—with a year's supply valued at $7,000. A month later, the company was forced to reduce the cost by 20 percent.

Pharmaceutical companies claim that treatment costs are high to cover the research and development required to manufacture a drug. However, salaries,

A worker at Cipla's manufacturing outlet packages antiretroviral drugs for the treatment of HIV. The cost of treatment varies from country to country.

publicity, and advertising are thought to swallow a large percentage of the profits. Fortunately, the cost of antiretroviral treatments in LEDCs has dropped dramatically in recent years. A year's supply costing several hundred U.S. dollars, can, in some places, now be offered for as little as $148.

Increased Competition

An increase in the production of generic drugs is one important contributing factor

 May 2000 Five pharmaceutical companies offer to heavily reduce the price of HIV drugs for Africa and other poor regions >>>

June 2000 The U.S.A. offers loans to sub-Saharan African nations to finance the cost of HIV treatments—the offer is rejected by many >>>

to declining costs. In 2001, 39 pharmaceutical companies took the South African government to court for buying cheaper generic HIV drugs from Cipla, a company based in India. But the court case was dropped after intense pressure from international aid agencies who argued that trade laws should not prevent the distribution of life-saving medication. That same year, an international agreement was reached at a World Trade Organization (WTO) meeting in Doha, Qatar, to make cheap HIV drugs available to all.

But controversies over treatment costs still continue. In 2007, for example, Cipla was investigated for a 150 percent price difference between antiretroviral treatments offered to African and Indian buyers. The problem of drug resistance is also a concern. While cheap generic drugs may offer a short-term solution, if strains of HIV become resistant to the drugs, thousands may then be denied access to new, more expensive, medication.

Antiretroviral drugs are developing all the time. These HIV treatments can be taken as three separate pills (top) or a combined pill (below). Generic drugs are much cheaper than their branded counterparts. In 2004, the combined (generic) drug shown here was $270 per patient per year, while the three separate drugs cost $560 per patient.

Clinical Trials

The only way to test the safety and effectiveness of a drug is to conduct clinical trials. Preclinical testing in a laboratory and on animals can determine whether a drug would be effective on humans, but human testing is vital before a drug can go on the market. During these tests, some volunteers are given a placebo so that a comparison can be properly trialled. Although there are safety concerns about the drugs being tested, those who are offered a placebo are also putting their lives at risk because they are not being treated.

2001 Cipla offers cheaper HIV drugs to Medecins Sans Frontieres (MSF). This puts pressure on other pharmaceutical companies to reduce their prices >>>

2001 39 companies halt their court case against the South African government's use of cheaper generic drugs to treat HIV >>>

33

Case Study: Marty St. Clair, who Discovered the First HIV Treatment

In November 1984, Marty St. Clair was running HIV drug trials for her company Burroughs Wellcome when she realized that azidothymidine (AZT) was having an effect against the virus. It was the kind of breakthrough any scientist dreams of. After much painstaking work, she had witnessed the effects of a drug that could reduce the death rate of people around the world.

Hope for the Future

Today, it takes up to ten years for a new drug to come on the market, but AZT was made available within three years. People were dying from AIDS, and the world welcomed any drug that might save them.

AZT was the first treatment found to have an effect against HIV.

AZT was not a cure for AIDS, but it helped to stem the progression of HIV. It had its drawbacks, however. The drug had severe side effects in some people and within a year, many patients began developing resistance to the treatment. But what AZT did achieve, was hope for the future. At last it seemed the effects of HIV could be tackled with science.

Friend or Foe?

Despite their continued efforts to find a treatment and cure for HIV, pharmaceutical companies have received bad press in the 25-year-battle against AIDS. High drug prices, particularly in poorer nations, have brought accusations of profiteering and greed. African nations have even accused Western governments of creating HIV for their own political and financial gain.

There is no doubt that AIDS has brought immense opportunities for pharmaceutical companies to develop their business, but most companies have now agreed to cut the price of their treatments and offer reasons for maintaining appropriate price bands. As HIV continues to spread indiscriminately, it has also become clear that the burden of AIDS cannot lie solely with the provision of treatments. Attitudes must change, too.

September 1986 Clinical trials show that azidothymidine (AZT) could slow the effects of HIV >>>

1995 A clinical trial proves that a combination of drugs is effective against HIV. The treatment becomes known as Highly Active Antiretroviral Therapy (HAART) >>>

WHAT THE WORLD THINKS...

These are three different publications commenting on AZT and the pharmaceutical industry's role in the fight against AIDS. Compare and contrast the various viewpoints and see if you can find any more newspaper reports or other media discussing HIV treatment.

The Post-Standard, Syracuse, New York, April 21, 2001

"'We are not the Red Cross,' [executive vice president of Pfizer Inc] said. 'We are a for-profit company.' In the last year, pharmaceutical companies have slashed the price of AIDS drugs for African countries. In so doing, executives...worry they might be undermining the patents that are the linchpin of their highly profitable industry. And just as frightening is the prospect of activists for other diseases using the AIDS drug offers as a lever to pry out similar concessions. There are other risks—that the drugs will be diverted to a black [illegal] market or that distribution problems in Africa will lead to a stronger strain of the virus.

"Pharmaceutical executives say it's time that other sectors of society took responsibility for the crisis. They note African governments have been slow to respond to their offers and the international community is doing little to build the infrastructure needed to combat the epidemic...There are other issues besides the price of drugs to be addressed."

AllAfrica Global Media web site, November 29, 2007

"Clearly...the virus was artificially created to target the Black race in particular. Some researchers...[claim] a cure has been found and is being kept a secret. Instead they promote the use of [antiretroviral drugs] that don't cure AIDS, but instead, earn mountains of money for the pharmaceutical companies."

BBC News 24 web site, UK, December 1, 2007

"There were complaints AZT was expensive and could have toxic side effects. But it offered hope. Not of a cure, but at least of a longer life for [those people] living with [HIV]. [The drug] cost $188 for 100 pills—out of reach for many people. 'It was frustrating,' Ms. St. Clair confesses. 'But we were doing our very best to make it available as easily as we could.

"'I do believe that where you are born shouldn't determine the quality of your healthcare,' said Ms. St. Clair. 'Our company has really made inroads into making drugs available for patients in developing nations.'"

AIDS and the Media

Whatever scientific breakthroughs the future brings, communication is the most important weapon in our fight against HIV and AIDS. And responsible media coverage plays a vital part in this process. While the media can spread educational messages around the globe, it can also relay inaccurate information and reinforce people's prejudices.

The Power of the Media

The media influences many aspects of our lives, reporting on daily events, shaping people's attitudes, and providing a source of education. In the 1980s, frightening headlines and widespread advertising campaigns attracted the world's attention to AIDS. But today, a new generation is growing up with little knowledge of the disease. Alarmingly, young people (under 25 years of age) now account for half of all new HIV infections worldwide.

Changing Headlines

Over the past 25 years, our perceptions of AIDS and HIV have changed dramatically. Once reported as a "death sentence" and largely a gay problem,

*Mohammed Farrouk (center), who is HIV positive, hosts the **AIDS On Line** television show in Nigeria. It is shown weekly to educate and inform the public about HIV and AIDS.*

 January 1991 Requests for HIV testing increase in the UK after the character Mark Fowler (from the popular UK soap *Eastenders*) is diagnosed with HIV >>>

November 1991 Freddie Mercury, singer of the rock group Queen, announces he has AIDS just before his death >>>

AIDS has now become a "chronic disease" affecting all walks of life, but one that can be easily managed.

Once in a while, the threat resurfaces, when a celebrity endorses a campaign, when someone famous dies, or when governments are called into question. But as every year goes by, "AIDS fatigue" brings the risk of the pandemic becoming old news. There is renewed hope, however, that recent interest in international issues, such as the environment and fair trade, will help to bring AIDS the attention it deserves.

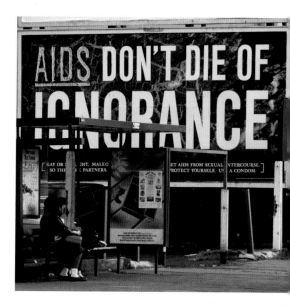

In 1987, AIDS awareness in the UK was at its height with a powerful advertising campaign across the country.

because treatment is now available. The international focus of some reports also encourages people in the West to presume that HIV cannot directly affect them, bringing a danger of complacency.

QUOTE >

"I think sometimes we think, well, only gay people can get it—it is not going to happen to me. And here I am saying that it can happen to anyone, even me, Magic Johnson."

American basketball player **Earvin (Magic) Johnson**, "Magic Johnson ends his career, saying he has AIDS infection," *New York Times*, November 8, 1991.

Misunderstandings

Stories that sensationalize the severity of HIV are the most stigmatizing of all, widening the divide between those who are, and those who are not, infected. At the other end of the spectrum, a decline in coverage seems to imply that HIV is not an issue any more, perhaps

Use of Language

The use of appropriate language is vital when talking about a disease such as AIDS. Misperceptions can be reinforced just by the tone or choice of words used. To describe someone as "an HIV sufferer," for example, implies that someone living with HIV is helpless and unable to live a full and active life. Our understanding of the causes of infection can also be undermined. To say that "she/he caught HIV" implies that the virus is spread by casual contact, even if this was not the sentiment intended.

1997 AIDS deaths begin to decline in MEDCs, thanks to new drugs >>>

1999 Heterosexual sex takes over from homosexual sex as the main transmitter of new HIV infections in the UK >>>

Case Study: Sarah Porter, Prosecuted for Reckless HIV Transmission

In June 2006, Sarah Porter, a woman from London, UK, was charged with GBH for the "reckless transmission of HIV." When an ex-boyfriend complained to the police, an investigation saw Sarah's home raided and her medical records checked. The police tracked down some of Sarah's other sexual partners, and one (who had HIV) filed an official complaint. Sarah was tried and sent to prison for 32 months.

A Fair Punishment?

Many AIDS organizations oppose the criminalization of reckless HIV transmission. They say that prosecutions and negative media reports add to the stigma that prevents people being tested for HIV and/or disclosing their HIV status.

Sarah was undoubtedly wrong to hide the fact she had HIV from her sexual partners—and any HIV infection she caused was devastating. But the responsibility of practicing safer sex lies with both parties. The first person in a relationship to be diagnosed with HIV is also not necessarily the first to be infected.

When Sarah was first diagnosed, she may not have received the support and advice she needed about disclosing her HIV status to others. Sarah may have been in denial about having HIV, fearing rejection if she told her family and friends.

Bold Assumptions

Some media reports implied the case was one of "deliberate" HIV transmission. Sarah was putting her partners at an extremely high risk, but it is doubtful she wanted to deliberately wreck their lives. Since 2003, there have been a number of prosecutions in the UK for the reckless transmission of HIV, under Section 20 of the Offenses Against the Person Act 1861. To date in the UK, however, there have been no prosecutions of deliberate transmission, which can carry a life sentence.

Sarah Porter was one of the first women prosecuted for the reckless transmission of HIV. But were the charges against her fair?

April 1989 A Dutch man with HIV is jailed in Minnesota under a new law banning people with HIV from entering the U.S.A. >>>

1999 A U.S. doctor who injected his former lover with HIV-infected blood is sentenced to 50 years in prison >>>

38

WHAT THE WORLD THINKS...

These are three different publications commenting on Sarah Porter's conviction in 2006. Compare and contrast the various viewpoints and see if you can find any more newspaper reports or other media discussing the case or the media's reporting of similar prosecutions.

The Times, UK, June 20, 2006

"Porter...wept throughout the hearing as the court was told of the suffering she had caused her former partner. The man, referred to as Mr. C, attempted suicide after his diagnosis, and, in an impact statement, said that he felt betrayed and told how the life he planned had ended. He felt numb, was in shock, and knew that there was a 'time bomb living inside him.' He said that Porter might have been motivated by revenge.

"Porter herself was a victim. She was infected by another partner so I can understand people thinking that revenge was a motive, but she never told us."

The Daily Mail, UK, June 20, 2006

"Mr. C...added: 'Sarah was pure evil in my eyes...' The police have issued an appeal for anyone who may have slept with her since the 1990s. They said that Porter, who has stubbornly refused to name any of her partners, is thought to have had unprotected sex with dozens of men she met at nightclubs in major cities."

The Independent on Sunday, UK, June 22, 2006

"Detective Sergeant Brian McClusky told journalists that he could not comprehend why Ms. Porter had 'set about this deliberate chain of events...revenge might have been one possible motive.'

"The full facts suggest a different picture...The man who turned out to be HIV-positive was...having sex with more than one other woman at the time.

"Ms. Porter did not insist on unprotected sex on every occasion... She chose, as was her right, to answer 'no comment' to all police questions, a fact that has given rise to unfair stories which imply that she refused to help the police to trace her lovers...Her plight is a disaster for everyone working with AIDS."

 2001 Scotsman Stephen Kelly becomes the first person to be prosecuted in the UK for the reckless transmission of HIV >>>

April 2007 Giovanni Mola, an Italian waiter working in Scotland, is sentenced to nine years in prison for the reckless transmission of HIV and hepatitis C >>>

Keeping the Message Alive

With AIDS reports now spanning over a quarter of a century, campaigners need to find new ways to hold the public's interest. With so many other issues clamouring for attention, this can be a struggle. Big-impact stories, such as natural disasters, are prone to grab the headlines, despite the fact that AIDS claims far more lives.

In 1988, the introduction of World AIDS Day helped to redress this balance. Every year on December 1, an annual themed day helps to raise awareness of HIV and AIDS. This is an opportune time to attract attention, but there is also the risk of high-profile coverage being limited to a single day, and then forgotten.

Access to Information

In some countries, public health messages are rarely heard. Cultural taboos about sexuality discourage access to information. Language barriers, illiteracy, and the logistics of media channels reaching remote locations are also a problem. But on the positive side, local radio stations with talk shows and call-ins are proving to be an effective source of information, with an added opportunity for people to get their voices heard.

Movies and television programs, such as *Soul City*—South Africa's most popular

Community media is proving to be a vital tool in the fight against AIDS, with the radio becoming the single most important channel of communication in Africa.

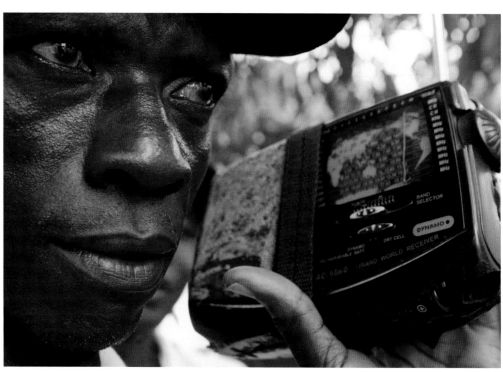

March 1987 ACT UP (the AIDS Coalition to Unleash Power) is founded to campaign for people living with HIV. They hold their first mass demonstration on Wall Street, New York City >>>

1991 The red ribbon becomes an international symbol of AIDS awareness >>>

Members of ACT UP wear masks representing former UK Prime Minister Tony Blair (right) and former French President Jacques Chirac (left) as they protest for more AIDS funding during an international conference in Paris.

soap opera, reaching approximately 30 million people across nine African nations—have also helped to spread important messages. The strong AIDS awareness themes in these programs are making a difference and producers have been inspired to expand this so-called "edutainment," helped by a $127 million investment by the U.S. Agency for International Development.

Changing Times

With increasing technology, cell phones, web sites, blogs, and forums have now joined traditional media channels. This new media is often unchecked, bringing the risk of misrepresentation, but it also provides opportunities for people

living with HIV to access support and advice and to air their views anonymously. When information is spread between communities, messages are also reinforced, giving validity to the information.

Powerful Voices

Political activism has also helped to draw the world's attention to the AIDS crisis. South Africa's Treatment Action Campaign (TAC), for example, infamously challenged the government's opposition to antiretroviral drugs. Protests in South African cities (which included threats to bring the dead bodies of activists who had died from AIDS to the demonstrations) were highly publicized around the world, putting intense pressure on the South African government to respond. In the United States, too, activist groups such as ACT UP have disrupted AIDS conferences with their protests, adding to high-profile media stories.

 March 1994 The American actor Tom Hanks wins an Oscar for playing a homosexual man with HIV in the film *Philadelphia* >>>

December 2007 British singer Annie Lennox releases a charity record to raise money and awareness for TAC >>>

What Does the Future Hold?

AIDS has now dominated our lives for over a quarter of a century. Despite a greater understanding of the cause of the disease, and medical advancements in treatment and prevention, we have been unable to stop the pandemic. But there have also been major success stories that give us real hope for the future.

A Long-Term Solution

A continued increase in levels of HIV infection has taught us that the fight against AIDS is a long-term strategy. Governments need to actively support initiatives so that the people most affected are supported and encouraged to change behaviors and attitudes in the long run. And these messages need to be passed to each generation.

AIDS is a global concern, but the most successful interventions have taken place within the context of each country. While we need to learn from each other, every nation also needs to find its own approach to tackling the disease. The response has been most effective in countries with open

These children have lost many friends and relatives to AIDS. But with the help of the international community, there is hope that their lives could one day be free from HIV.

October 1987 AIDS becomes the first disease to be debated by the United Nations (UN) General Assembly >>>

January 1996 The Joint United Nations Program on AIDS (UNAIDS) is established >>>

channels of communication, where changes in sexual behavior are accompanied by a deeper social change. By encouraging public debate, the media can play an important part in challenging established social norms.

How Long Will it Take?

There have been major breakthroughs in the types and cost of treatment, transforming the world's response to HIV and AIDS. But most scientists do not expect a widely available vaccine or cure for the virus within a decade. Instead, it is expected to take at least 20 years to make an impact on the disease.

In the meantime, treatment costs need to be reduced, local healthcare provision requires heavy investment, but, most of all, people need to take responsibility for their sexual health and attitudes must change.

Sustaining Activity

In the 1980s, the gay community in the U.S.A. mobilized a political response to AIDS, bringing the crisis to the world's attention. More recently, groups such as the TAC have brought changes in Africa, too. This level of public motivation needs to be sustained if governments are to make a difference. In the West, there is a danger that complacency is setting in

> QUOTE >

"In this effort, there is no 'us and them,' no developed and developing countries, no rich and poor—only a common enemy that knows no frontiers and threatens all people."

Former UN Secretary **General Kofi Annan** at the G8 summit in Genoa, Italy, July 20, 2001.

Researchers have been battling with HIV for over 25 years. A cure for the disease is proving difficult to find, but each day we're a step closer to meeting the challenge.

because treatments are beginning to improve the situation. AIDS is a concern for all of us and there is no time like the present to act—whoever we are, and wherever we live.

May 1997 President Clinton sets a target for U.S.A. to find an AIDS vaccine within ten years. This aim is unmet >>>

2004 The U.S.A. launches a major initiative called PEPFAR to combat AIDS worldwide >>>

Case Study: Michel Sidibé, Executive Director of UNAIDS

On December 1, 2009, World AIDS Day saw global campaigns and events drawing attention to the plight of AIDS sufferers. UNAIDS Executive Director Michel Sidibé urged leaders at all levels of society to hold focus in the battle against HIV, to ensure that positive progress was maintained.

UNAIDS' Michel Sidibé is leading international efforts in the fight against HIV and AIDS.

A Turning Point?

Since the first World AIDS Day in 1988, the percentage of the world's population living with HIV has finally stabilized. But there is a long way to go—estimates claim that every day there are more than 6,800 new HIV infections, and over 5,700 deaths to AIDS—alarming statistics.

But at last, the world is beginning to pull together. In 2006, UN member states agreed targets for universal access to HIV prevention, treatment, care, and support. Access to antiretroviral treatment is increasing in sub-Saharan Africa, HIV infections are falling in many countries, and around 30 new vaccines are being tested.

Where Do We Go from Here?

Funding is a major issue for the future. If UN targets on HIV and AIDS are to be achieved, for example, approximately $20 billion a year is needed. Issues of stigma and discrimination also need to be tackled urgently to ensure that people take responsibility for their sexual health and complacency is avoided.

In September 2006, the pharmaceutical company Merck stopped human trials of an HIV vaccine because there were worries that it might increase the risk of infection to those exposed to the virus. It was a huge blow to the research effort. But while the search for a safe and effective vaccine goes on, improved antiretroviral treatments offer quality of life to those infected and there are renewed hopes that microbicides could soon be available. It has taken more than 25 years, but the victory over AIDS is surely within our grasp.

December 1, 1988 The first World AIDS Day takes place. People around the world are urged to "Join the worldwide effort" >>>

1999 The WHO reports that AIDS has become the fourth biggest killer worldwide >>>

WHAT THE WORLD THINKS...

These are three different publications commenting on World AIDS Day. Compare and contrast the various viewpoints and see if you can find any more newspaper reports or other media discussing the future of AIDS.

Michel Sidibé, UNAIDS press statement, December 1, 2009

"On this World AIDS Day, we are filled with both hope and concern. Hope because significant progress has been made toward universal access. New HIV infections have dropped. Fewer children are born with HIV. And more than 4 million people are on treatment. Concern because 28 years into the epidemic, the virus continues to make inroads into new populations; stigma and discrimination continue to undermine efforts to turn back the epidemic. "

USA Today, December 1, 2009

"President Jacob Zuma...declared Tuesday in a national address on World AIDS Day that drug therapy for HIV-positive pregnant women and babies would be broadened and start earlier. Mr. Zuma's approach on Tuesday...won him wide praise from the advocates who had despaired under Mr. Mbeki."

Daily Planet, Minnesota December 3, 2009

"There are currently 6,220 people living with HIV and AIDS in Minnesota and an estimated 2,500 people are believed to be living with HIV without knowing their status.

"Dave Folken, from the Minnesota AIDS Project, suggests that one of the reasons for HIV increase is a surge of new infections in different demographics including young people. They did not receive the first round of public awareness campaigns when young adults grew up knowing and understanding AIDS.

"Folken says that young people, and others, do not realize that AIDS is still a very dangerous disease. 'They think that HIV is like other sexually transmitted diseases,' he says, 'that it is treatable and not a big deal.'"

2001 189 members of the UN sign a Declaration of Commitment on HIV and AIDS pledging to reduce HIV infection among young people (age 15 to 24) by 25 percent in the most affected countries by 2005, and to reduce it globally by 25 percent by 2010 >>>

ACT UP AIDS Coalition to Unleash Power is a U.S. activist group seeking to end the AIDS crisis. ACT UP protests have brought widespread media attention.

adherence Continuing a course of treatment as prescribed by a doctor, despite difficulties with side effects or methods of application.

anonymous When someone withholds their identity to remain unknown.

antibodies Proteins formed by the immune system to protect the body against foreign substances, such as bacteria and viruses.

antiretroviral Drugs used to treat retrovirus infections, such as HIV.

apartheid A political system in South Africa in the twentieth century in which black people were denied basic rights and freedoms.

AZT Azidothymidine is the first antiretroviral treatment found to slow the progression of HIV.

bird flu A type of influenza affecting birds, which has transferred to humans in some cases and has caused death in some parts of Asia.

bisexual A person who is sexually attracted to people of both sexes.

Black Death A type of plague that affected Europe and Asia in the fourteenth century.

blood transfusion The process of transferring blood from one person to another, for medical reasons.

Caesarean birth An operation used to deliver a baby.

CDC The Centers for Disease Control and Prevention is a U.S. government agency working to promote health and quality of life by preventing and controlling disease, injury, and disability.

chronic disease A disease that is long-lasting.

circumcision The surgical removal of the foreskin of the penis for medical or religious reasons.

complacency When people are content, but unaware of the dangers involved.

contagious A disease that can spread from one person to another through surface-to-skin contact or through the air.

discrimination When someone is treated unfairly because they are seen to belong to a particular group.

epidemic A widespread disease.

euthanasia Helping someone to end their life, because they have a terminal disease or an incurable condition.

FDA The Food and Drug Administration is a U.S. government agency working to protect public health by assuring the safety, effectiveness, and accessibility of food supplies and medical treatments.

GBH Grievous bodily harm. GBH is an offense that can be prosecuted in a court of law.

generic drug A copy of a brand-name drug that is made by another company at reduced cost.

HAART Highly active antiretroviral therapy. A combination of several (usually three or four) antiretroviral drugs used to treat HIV.

hemophiliac Someone with a genetic disease (usually affecting males) that prevents the blood clotting effectively, to heal wounds.

hepatitis C A blood-borne infectious disease that infects the liver. Some people with HIV may have contracted hepatitis C, caused by the hepatitis C virus (HCV).

heterosexual A person who is sexually attracted to people of the opposite sex.

HIV Human Immunodeficiency Virus is a virus that can lead to AIDS. Two strains of HIV have been identified—HIV-1 and HIV-2. HIV-1 is the cause of most HIV infections, and is more easily transmitted. At the moment, HIV-2 is mainly confined to West Africa.

homophobia Disapproval or discrimination against homosexuals.

homosexual A person who is sexually attracted to people of the same sex.

immune system The way the body protects itself against bacteria, viruses, and other infections.

KS Kaposi's Sarcoma is a type of cancer commonly occurring in AIDS patients.

LEDCs Less Economically Developed Countries are the poorer countries of the world, including the countries of Africa, Asia (except Japan), Latin America, and the Caribbean.

MEDCs More Economically Developed Countries are the richer countries of the world, including Europe, northern North America, and Australia.

microbicides Substances used as a barrier to prevent the transmission of viruses.

mutate To change to another form.

pandemic A disease affecting a whole country, or the world.

PCP Pneumocystis carinii pneumonia is a lung infection commonly occurring in AIDS patients.

PEP Post Exposure Prophylaxis is a preventative treatment. PEP is sometimes given after exposure to HIV (or suspected exposure) to decrease the chances of an HIV infection.

pharmaceutical company A company that researches, develops, markets, and/or distributes drugs, mostly in the context of healthcare. Examples include: Burroughs Wellcome (the company behind the first antiretroviral treatment for HIV); Cipla (one of the world's largest manufacturers of antiretroviral drugs); Pfizer (one of the world's largest research-based pharmaceutical companies); and GlaxoSmithKline (formed by a series of mergers of Burroughs Wellcome, Glaxo Laboratories, Beecham, and SmithKline Beckman).

placebo A substance containing no medication, used as a control during experiments to test the effectiveness of a drug.

racism A belief that people from different parts of the world have different characters or abilities, often leading to discrimination.

SARS A type of virus known as Severe Acute Respiratory Syndrome that began in Asia and the Far East in 2003.

sensationalize To describe something in an extreme way to make it more noticeable.

Spanish flu A severe and deadly form of influenza affecting people around the world in the aftermath of World War I. It received greatest media attention in Spain, hence its name.

stigma A form of prejudice against an individual or a group because they are thought to be different to other people.

sub-Saharan Africa African countries that are found south of the Sahara Desert.

taboo Something that is forbidden because of cultural beliefs.

TAC Treatment Action Campaign is a South African AIDS activist organization that campaigns for greater access to HIV treatment.

UN The United Nations is an organization of nations, formed in 1945 to promote peace, security, and international cooperation.

vaccination A method of preventing infectious diseases. Vaccinations introduce a bacteria or virus into the body (usually by way of a needle) to encourage the immune system to develop resistance to a disease.

Vatican The papal government, head of the Roman Catholic Church.

WHO The World Health Organization is the United Nations agency for health.

WTO The World Trade Organization is an international organization dealing with the rules of trade between nations.

Index

Numbers in **bold** refer to illustrations.

ACT UP 40, 41, **41**, 46
antibodies 16, 26, 46
antiretroviral drugs/treatment 6, 7, 13, 16, 19, 26, 28, 30, 33, **33**, 35, 41, 44, 46, 47
Ashe, Arthur 15
AZT (azidothymidine) 7, 30, 32, 34, **34**, 35, 46

bird flu 8, 46
bisexual 12, 46
Black Death 8, 46
blood transfusion 13, 14, 15, 46
Brazil 28
breastfeeding 13

Catholic Church 13
CDC 4–5, 7, 10, 11, 46
childbirth 13, 46
chimpanzees 9, 12
China 28, 29
Cipla **32**, 33, 47
clean needles 25
clinical trials 33
condom 7, 12, 21, 26, 29, 31
Curran, Dr. James 10–11

discrimination 14, 18, 20, 21, 44, 45, 46
drug user 4, 10, 12, 13
Durban Declaration, the 31

economic impact 18
education 15, 19, 20, 21, 23, 24, **25**, 28, 36

FDA 7, 21, 46
fear 14, 20
financial impact 6

generic drugs 32, 33, **33**, 46
Global AIDS Fund 33

HAART 16, 34, 46
Haiti 9, 10
hemophilia 12, **14**, 14–15, 46
heterosexual 12, 25, 26, 28, 37, 44, 46
homophobia 21, 46
homosexual 4, 10, 11, 12, 25, 28, 37, 41, 44, 46, 47
human cost 18

India 18, 21, 22, 23, 33

Kaposi's Sarcoma 10, 47

LEDCs 19, 21, 24, 25, 28, 32, 47

malaria **8**
Marabe, Margaret 22–23
Mbeki, President Thabo 28, **30**, 30–31
media 21, 24, 36–41, **37**, **40**
microbicides 6, 26, 27, 44, 47

origins 12
orphans 6, 18

pandemic 4, 12, 19, 37, 47
Papua New Guinea **22**, 22–23
PEP 16, 47
pharmaceutical companies 32, 33, 34, 35, 47
political influences 7
Porter, Sarah 38–39
pregnancy 13
prejudice 21, 36
prevention 6, 8, 12, 18, 26, 42, 44, 48
Princess Diana 7

racism 21, 47
Ray brothers, the 14–15
Ricky Ray Relief Fund Act, 1988 14

SARS 8, 29, 47
sex education 24, 25
sexual behavior 43
sexual health 20, 24, 26, 44
social influences 7
South Africa 25, 28, 30–31, 40, 41
St. Clair, Mary 34–35
sterilized needles 13
stigma 7, 20, 21, **21**, 23, 30, 38, 44, 45, 47
sub-Saharan Africa 5, 12, **13**, **19**, 21, 24, 32, 44, 47
symptoms 5, 10
syringe exchange program 12

TAC 41, 43, 47
Terence Higgins Trust 24
testing 14, 16, 24, 26, 30, 36
transmission 12, 13, 26, 38, 39, 47
treatment 5, 6, 7, 8, 16, 18, 25, 26, 27, 30, 33, 35, 42, 43, 48

UNAIDS 42, 48
unprotected sex 12, 39

vaccine 6, 17, **27**, 43, 44, 47
Vatican 13, 47

WHO 13, 23, 47
World AIDS Day 40, 44, 45, 48
WTO 33, 47

FURTHER INFORMATION AND WEB SITES

BOOKS

AIDS and HIV
by Rae Simons
(AlphaHouse Publishing, 2008)

HIV and AIDS
(Coping in a Changing World)
by Paula Johanson
(Rosen Publishing Group, 2007)

AIDS (Epidemics and Society)
by Molly Jones
(Rosen Publishing Group, 2010)

WEB SITES

Due to the changing nature of Internet links, Rosen Publishing has developed an online list of Web sites related to the subject of this book. This site is regularly updated. Please use this link to access this list: http://www.rosenlinks.com/glo/aids